Rory
and the
Monstersitter

Rosie Reeve

BLOOMSBURY

LONDON NEW DELHI NEW YORK SYDNEY

Rory **loved** to cook.

with a bit of help from
his dad, he made
blue pancakes
for breakfast...

cheese bats for lunch...

creepy crawly
buggy snacks...

...and **hairy cakes** for tea.

One evening, Mum and Dad decided to go out for dinner.

They ordered a babysitter for the children and went to get ready.

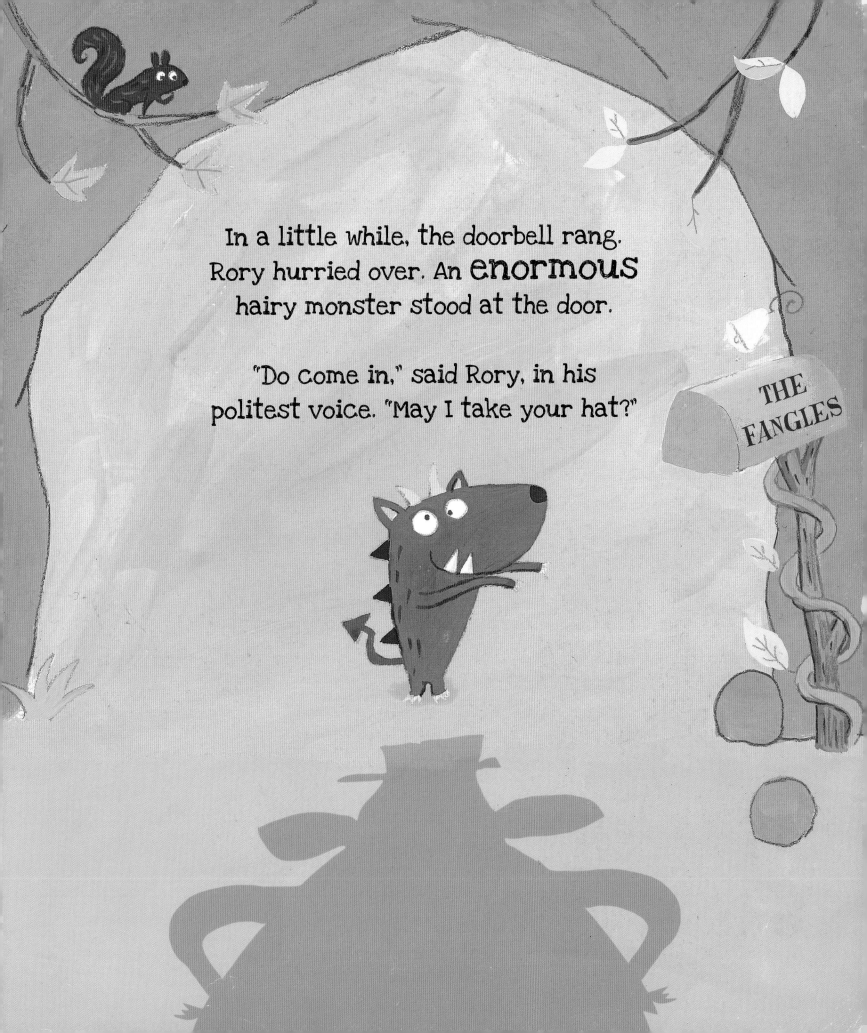

In a little while, the doorbell rang.
Rory hurried over. An **enormous**
hairy monster stood at the door.

"Do come in," said Rory, in his
politest voice. "May I take your hat?"

THE FANGLES

The huge, hairy monster grunted.
Then he stomped into the house, turned
on the TV and slumped on to the sofa.

The children went to play outside.

THE
FANGLES

Fangus and Lily collected
some sticks, while Rory
played with Baby Grub.

"Be good little monsters while we're out,"
said Mum and Dad, waving goodbye.
And they set off into the forest.

Once they were out of sight, Rory, Fangus, Lily and Baby Grub tiptoed into the house.

They sneaked past the babysitter and went into the kitchen.

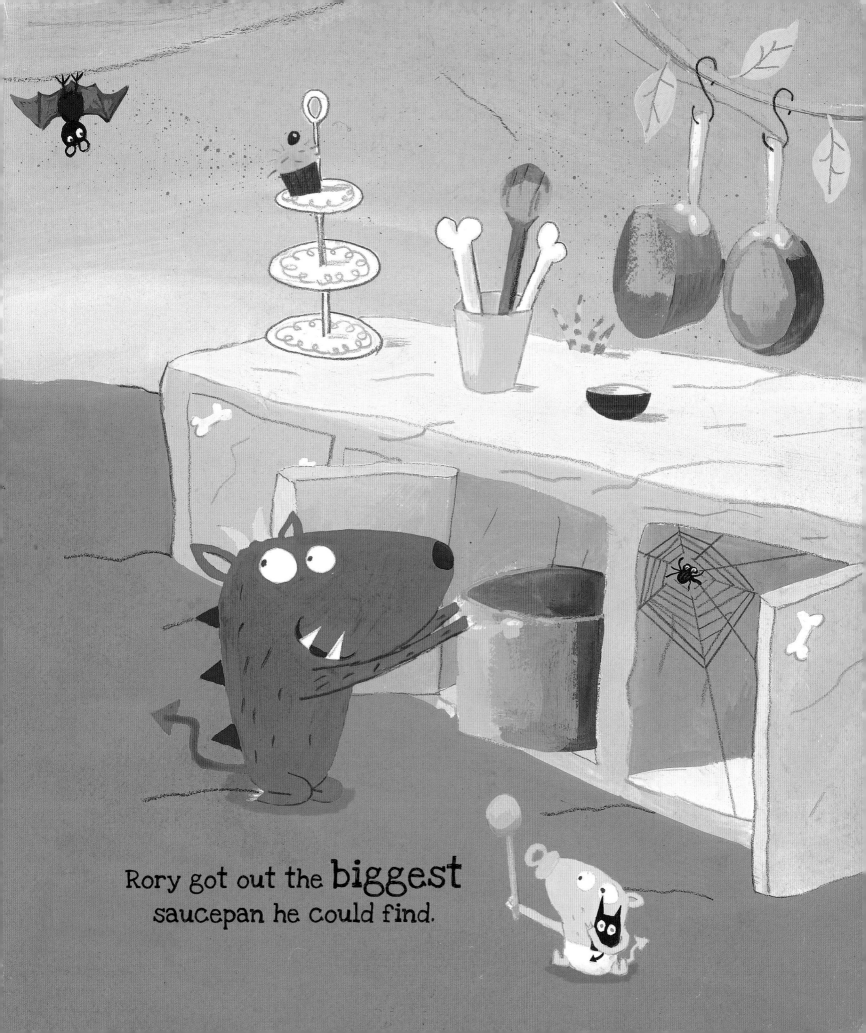

Rory got out the **biggest** saucepan he could find.

He dragged it outside and filled it with
leaves and twigs. He added a splash of water,
a twist of pepper and a sprinkling of salt.

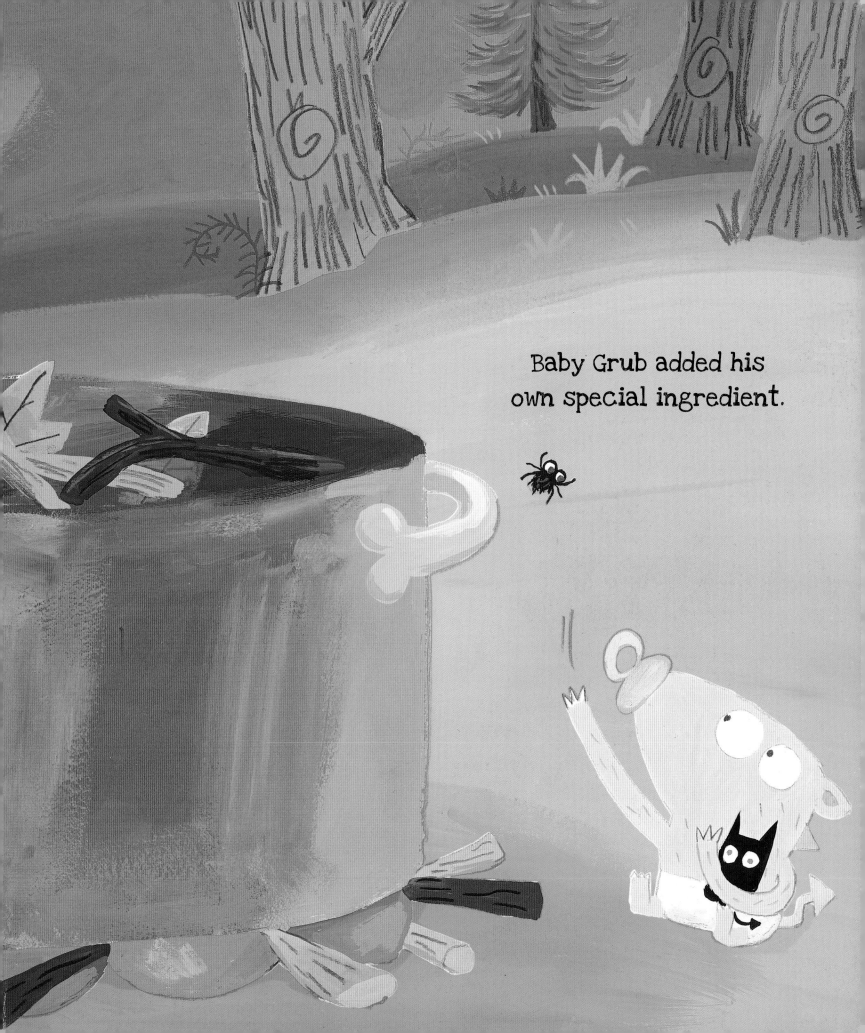

Baby Grub added his own special ingredient.

Not far away, Mum and Dad were having
dinner at the Cockroach Café.
They ate soup and soufflé and slimeball spaghetti.

Then they ordered puddings and coffee
and biscuits and cheese.

But back at home, tummies were rumbling.
Supper wasn't quite ready.

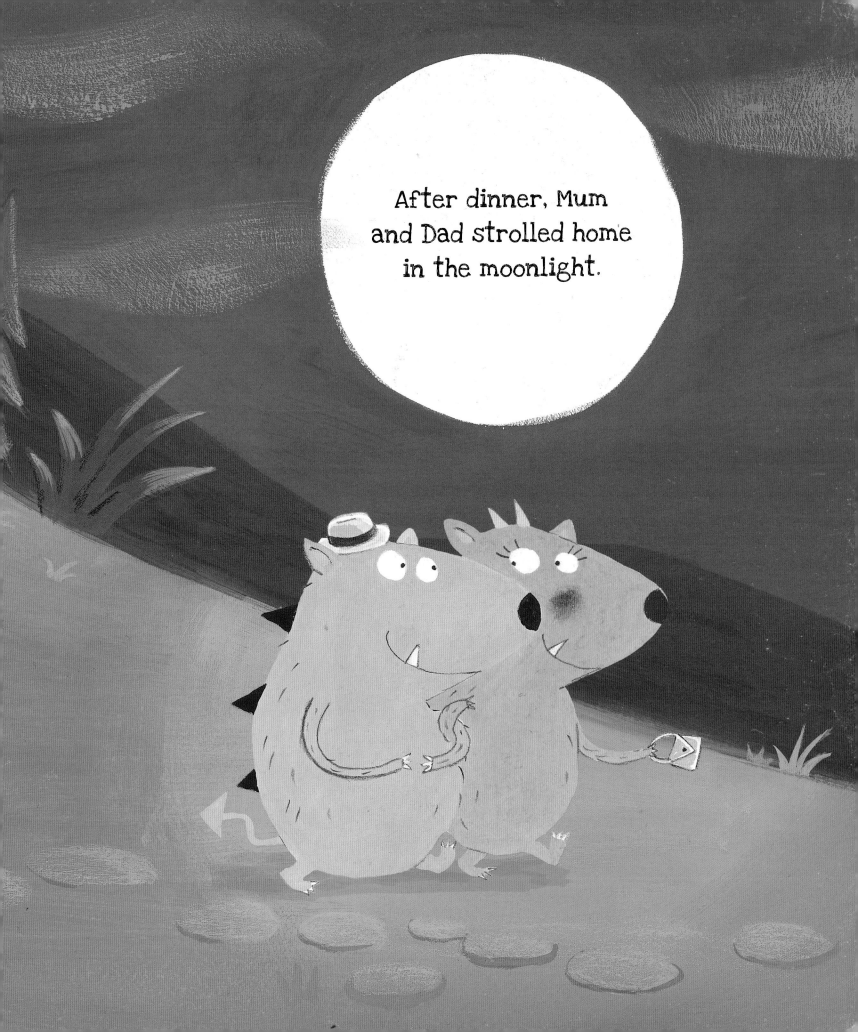

After dinner, Mum
and Dad strolled home
in the moonlight.

When they got back,
all was quiet...

The kitchen was
clean and tidy.

The twins were
snoring peacefully.

Baby Grub was fast asleep.

Only Rory was still awake.

"And how was the babysitter, dear?"
asked Mum and Dad.

The next morning, **everyone** was hungry again.

"Don't worry, my dears," said Mum,
"the postman will be here soon."

"YUM!" said Rory.
"I'll get the frying pan."

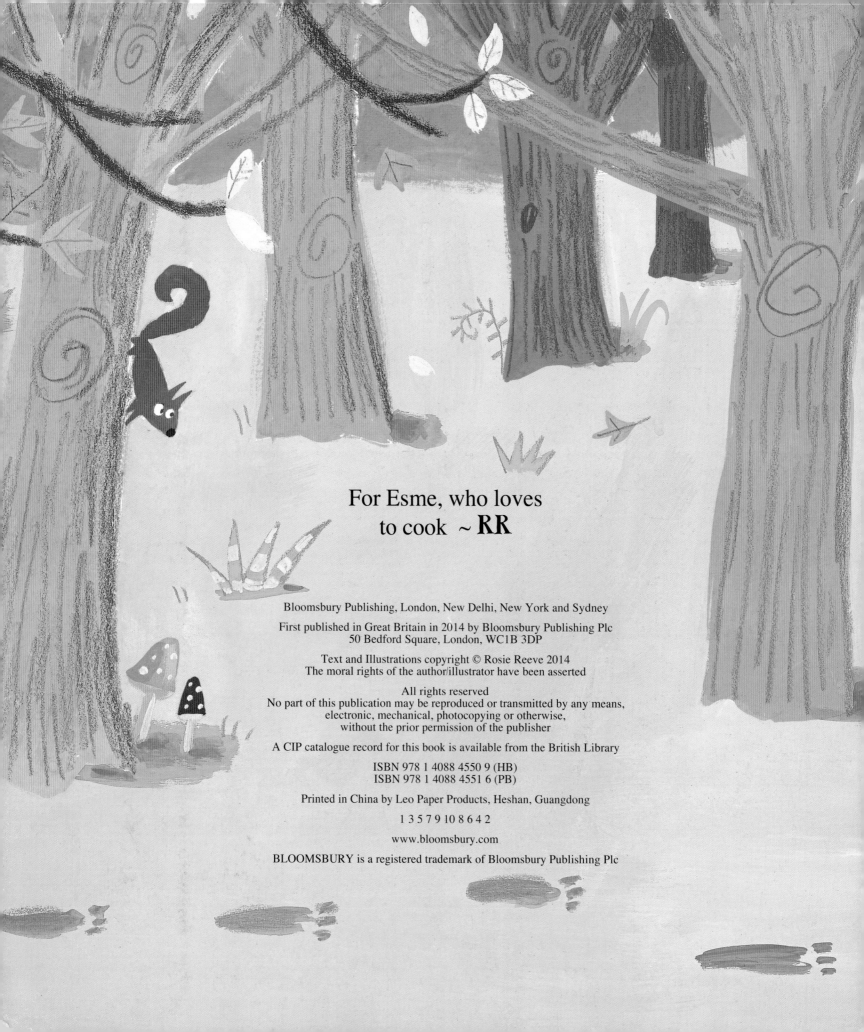

For Esme, who loves
to cook ~ **RR**

Bloomsbury Publishing, London, New Delhi, New York and Sydney

First published in Great Britain in 2014 by Bloomsbury Publishing Plc
50 Bedford Square, London, WC1B 3DP

Text and Illustrations copyright © Rosie Reeve 2014
The moral rights of the author/illustrator have been asserted

A CIP catalogue record for this book is available from the British Library

ISBN 978 1 4088 4550 9 (HB)
ISBN 978 1 4088 4551 6 (PB)

Printed in China by Leo Paper Products, Heshan, Guangdong

1 3 5 7 9 10 8 6 4 2

www.bloomsbury.com

BLOOMSBURY is a registered trademark of Bloomsbury Publishing Plc